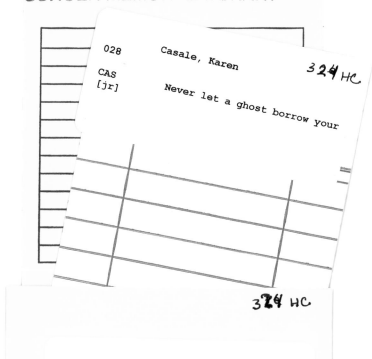

Never Let a Ghost Borrow Your Library Book

Book Care Guidelines from the Library Secret Service

Karen Casale

Illustrations by
Cecilia Rebora

UpstartBooks

Madison, Wisconsin
www.upstartbooks.com

To Tyler, Chris, Evan, and Dan with love. (Thanks for always taking good care of your library books!) And to Mom and Dad, for encouraging my love of reading.
—K. C.

For Ines, Mateo, and Teffy for so many nice afternoons and all the help.—C. R.

Published by UpstartBooks
4810 Forest Run Road
Madison, WI 53704
1-608-241-1201

Text © 2012 by Karen Casale
Illustrations © 2012 by Cecilia Rebora

The paper used in this publication meets the minimum requirements of American National Standard for Information Science — Permanence of Paper for Printed Library Material. ANSI/NISO Z39.48.

PROPERTY OF
THE LIBRARY
SECRET SERVICE

(Didn't even know there was
such a thing, did you?)

When you borrow a book from the library, you probably know that you can't keep it forever. Other kids want to borrow that book, too.

So while you have it, you must take care of it. For the next kid.

That's where the **LIBRARY SECRECT SERVICE (L.S.S.)** comes in.

The L.S.S. has issued **VERY OFFICIAL GUIDELINES (V.O.G.)** so that you know how to take care of your library book ...

Psssst! Turn the page!

V.O.G. #1 Let's start with pets. Do NOT let your pets eat library books. Examples of pets include dogs, cats, turtles, hamsters, and inchworms—basically anything that eats and burps.

V.O.G. #2 Do not let a baby drool on your books. Especially if he's just eaten strained peas. Do not let elves or ogres drool on them, either. They have very smelly drool.

V.O.G. #3 Do not drink or eat anything—especially the librarian's lunch—while reading a library book. Also, never drink alien juice next to your book. Alien juice stains.*

*CONFIRMED BY THE L.S.S. LAUNDRY DEPARTMENT

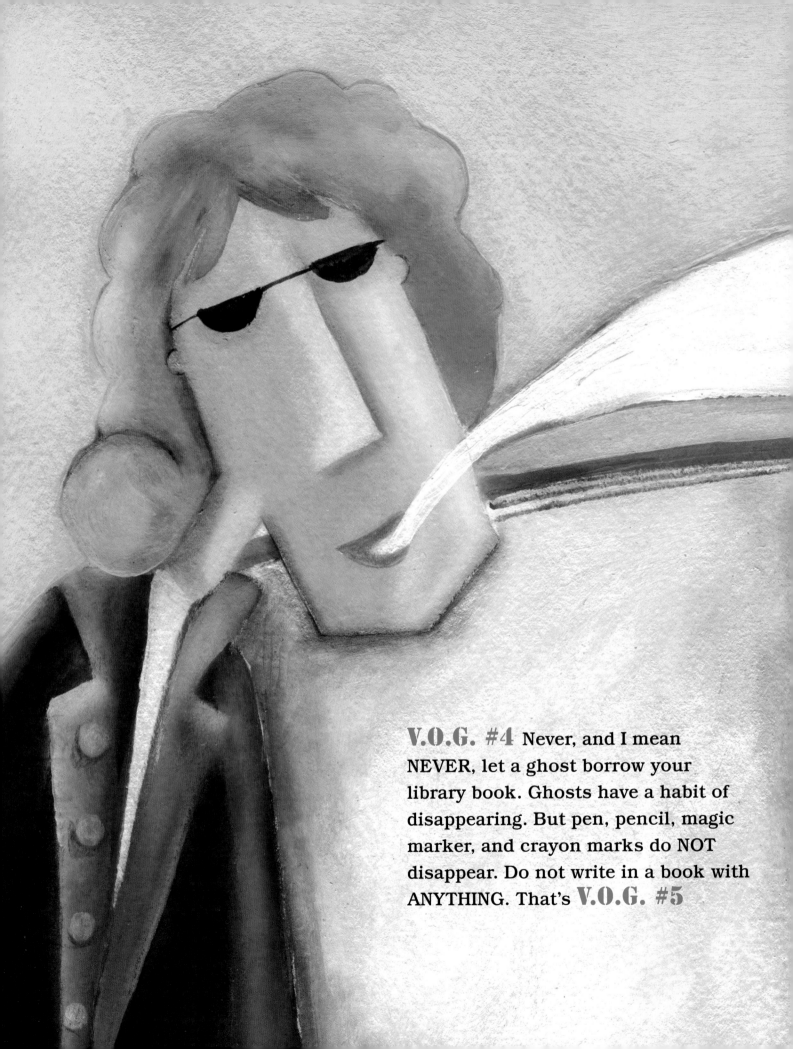

V.O.G. #4 Never, and I mean NEVER, let a ghost borrow your library book. Ghosts have a habit of disappearing. But pen, pencil, magic marker, and crayon marks do NOT disappear. Do not write in a book with ANYTHING. That's **V.O.G. #5**

V.O.G. #6

Do not take your books out in the rain or put them in the bathtub. *You* should definitely take a bath, however. The sooner, the better.

Rubber duck optional.

If you don't know what "optional" means, ask your librarian to help you LOOK IT UP in the reference section.

V.O.G. #7

Also, do not leave your books out in the sun. They are sensitive to UV rays, just like you. And no, sun block on books is **NOT** a good idea.

V.O.G. #8

Do not dog-ear, dog-slurp, or dog-slime your books. Use a bookmark! If you don't have one, use a slip of paper.

V.O.G. #9 Do not use your library book as a tissue or napkin. Do not make mud cakes and then touch your book, either. Please, we're begging you.

V.O.G. #10

DON'T

turnthepagestoofastbecausethenyou'llhearaterriblerippingsound!

Turn the pages slowly.

POP QUIZ!

Where is the best place to keep library books at home?

A. The hamper (with all your dirty, stinky socks)

B. The doghouse (an alien's favorite hangout)

C. The freezer (brrrrrrrrr!)

D. A bookcase, table, shelf, or somewhere else that's safe

Hope you picked "D."
That's **V.O.G. #12**

If you did, you're an honorary member of
the L.S.S. for the day!

V.O.G. #13 Hug your books when you carry them so you don't drop them. Or hug them because you love them soooooooo much! Whatever the reason, hug them to keep them safe.

V.O.G. #14

If you love a library book soooooo much that you want to keep it longer, renew it. But remember, you still can't kiss it, even if you love it soooooo much that you want to marry it.

If you love the book that much, ask someone to buy it for you. Then you can smooch it all you want.

Ask your mom, dad, Santa, grandma, the president, or your favorite movie star. Do NOT ask a vampire to buy a book for you. You don't want to be alone with a vampire.*

*CONFIRMED BY
L.S.S.
SECURITY FORCE

V.O.G. #15

Finally, and most important ... drum roll please ... **READ THE BOOK!** Read it to yourself, to your parents, to your sister, to your sister's smooshed-up sandwich, to your stuffed animals, to space aliens, to ants, to your mom's coffee cup, to your brother's freckle ... to anyone or anything. (Well, maybe not to a vampire. See V.O.G. #14.)

Oh, we almost forgot! V.O.G. #16

Remember to say thank you to the librarian. Your librarian cares for all those great books in the library that you love. And ALL librarians are members of the L.S.S.

(And pssst... they are glad that you love your books.)